Winx CLUB™

Dragon Fire

By
Michael
Anthony Steele

SCHOLASTIC INC.

ISBN 0-439-69151-6
Designed by Rocco Melillo

12 11 10 9 8 7 6 5 4 3 2 1   5 6 7 8 9/0

Printed in the U.S.A.
First printing, February 2005

Hi! My name is Bloom! I used to be a regular teenage girl whose biggest problem was how I was going to spend my summer vacation. Well, all that changed when I learned that fairies, witches, and magic really do exist! I even discovered that I have magical powers, too! Now I go to the Alfea School for Fairies to learn how to become the best fairy I can be!

I made tons of new friends at Alfea. In fact, five of us got together and formed the Winx Club. We're fairies with a passion for fashion and a flare for magic! But you know what? You don't have to go to a special school to learn all about fairies and witches. Just flip through this book and discover more about the enchanted land of Magix! You'll even get to read about one of my adventures!

The land of Magix

Here, magic is a powerful energy that springs from the essence of the world. Three different types of magic are taught in three different schools.

Alfea School for Fairies

At Alfea, teenage fairies from all over the universe enroll to improve their supernatural powers. New friends are made as they learn spells, enchanted auras, and magic potions.

Red Fountain School for Specialists

Red Fountain is the school where boys become specialists— skilled warriors and experts in battle strategies and tactics. They are heroes-in-training.

Cloud Tower School for Witches

At the evil Cloud Tower, the newest aspiring witches perfect their witchcraft in order to help the dark forces spread mischief to every corner of the universe.

Bloom
Fairy of Dragon Fire

Age: 16
Origin: Earth
Power Source: The mysterious Dragon Fire
Likes: Learning new spells; pizza with extra cheese.
Strengths: Bloom is independent, unselfish, and a born leader.
Weaknesses: She's somewhat impatient, stubborn, and a bit insecure due to the uncertain origin of her powers.

Bloom is one of the many girls who live on Earth with her friends, her dreams, and her problems. She loves her life but imagines the existence of another world, made of magical places and enchanted creatures.

Bloom quickly discovers that fantasy can turn to reality when she joins the other girls at the Alfea School for Fairies. As Bloom learns how to become a fairy, she realizes that she has great energy inside her. In fact, her destiny is very different from anything she could have ever imagined!

Kiko

Kiko is Bloom's clever pet bunny. He happily lives with Bloom in her dorm room at Alfea.

3

Stella
Fairy of Sun and Moon

Age: 17

Origin: Solaria

Power Source: The sun and moonlight

Likes: Stella likes all that is beautiful, love spells, and all the latest fashions.

Strengths: She's spirited, smart, and always stylish.

Weaknesses: Sometimes Stella is lazy and she's never very serious about schoolwork. She's also a compulsive shopper.

Stella came to Alfea because her parents wanted her to become a proper princess. However, she doesn't seem to care too much for school. Instead, she'd rather concentrate on her outfits and overall appearance.

She was also the one who found Bloom and coaxed her into becoming a fairy. Bloom enjoys Stella's lively character, but sometimes gets annoyed with her arrogance and huge ego. However, after becoming best friends with Bloom, Stella has begun to change the negative aspects of her character.

Flora
Fairy of Nature

Age: 16
Origin: The Fifth Moon of Marigold
Power Source: All flowers and plants
Likes: Flora enjoys forestry studies and botanical experiments.
Strengths: She is the most mature of the group and has a very responsible attitude.
Weakness: She lacks self-confidence.

Flora is Bloom's roommate. She is an affectionate girl who loves nature and is always helpful toward others. She is a mature and responsible student and her biggest dream is to learn to use her magical power to help all the plants and flowers of the Magic Dimension.

Sometimes her sensitivity makes her shy and insecure. She often lacks self-confidence, but with the support of her friends, she's slowly finding faith in her abilities.

5

Musa
Fairy of Music

Age: 16
Origin: The Harmonic Nebula
Power Source: All types of music
Likes: Musa loves to play musical instruments and to daydream.
Strengths: She's very athletic and she's a great dancer.
Weakness: She can have quite a temper, especially when absorbed by music that influences her moods.

Musa loves listening to music every chance she gets. In fact, the power she receives from music fills her with vitality and gives her an explosive personality. Her strength and creativity are often very helpful to her friends!

Although she is somewhat of a tomboy, she is very sensitive under her tough exterior. She is often moody, but is always ready to cheer up her friends in their most difficult moments.

Tecna
Fairy of Technology

Age: 16
Origin: The third vector of the binary galaxy.
Power Source: Tecna draws her power from all that is high-tech.
Likes: She adores all kinds of science and inventions.
Strengths: She's a perfectionist and is very decisive.
Weakness: Tecna is sometimes too confident.

Tecna has always felt a little different from her friends because of her love of science and inventions. While the other girls shop in their spare time, Tecna would rather make new discoveries and learn how things work.

Because of her determination and perfectionist personality, Tecna can appear emotionless and stern. Her friends know better and often value her wise advice. Tecna even surprises herself with the strong feelings she keeps deep inside.

The Witches

Icy
Heart of Ice

Energy Source: Ice
Deadly Powers: Freezing rain and icy darts
Motto: The Dragon Fire Power is mine!

Icy is the absolute leader of the witches. Thanks to her charisma and ability to twist the truth, she gets everyone to follow her and sometimes even convinces others to do her dirty work. She is extremely ambitious and will hurt anyone who gets in her way.

Darcy
Lady of Darkness

Energy Source: Darkness
Deadly Powers: Hypnotic wave and rays
Motto: No one can oppose us! The Winx's days are numbered!

Darcy is a witch who uses her hypnotic skills to confuse and deceive her opponents. She is very good at observing the behavior of others, finding their weaknesses, and then attacking them with her spellbinding look or with her distorting ray.

8

Stormy
Queen of Storms

Energy Source: Wind
Deadly Powers: Rising of gales and tempests
Motto: I will not go back to limbo without the Dragon Fire Power this time!

Stormy is a powerful witch who controls thunder, lightning, storms, and cyclones. She can shape wind and electricity to her will. She's at Cloud Tower because she wants to learn to master her turbulent powers perfectly. She has a bad temper and secretly believes that she's more powerful than Icy.

Knut

When this nearsighted ogre is not out running errands for Icy, he spends his time in Cloud Tower sweeping up, mixing potions, and generally being abused by the three witches.

The Specialists

Brandon

At Red Fountain, Brandon practices his swordsmanship, learns to ride dragons, and drives the latest techno-vehicles. He is brave and resourceful and always proves to be an avid and tenacious fighter who stops at nothing. He is the natural leader of his specialist friends.

Sky

Sky has trained for years in a training camp for soldiers. At Red Fountain, he perfects his remarkable fencing techniques at a higher level than other specialists. Other than sparring, he really likes girls. For this reason, he loves dressing very well. He's suave, debonair, and knows how to be a gentleman when it counts.

Riven

Riven is the shadowy one of the group. He is an excellent athlete and excels in all sports. Sometimes he's quite touchy and he never likes talking about himself or his private life. Riven also has a mysterious tie to the witches at Cloud Tower, particularly Darcy!

Timmy

Timmy comes from a family of scientists and researchers who are famous all over Magix for their original and innovative inventions. Timmy's particular expertise lies in combining technology and magic. He is quite resourceful and promptly finds the right solution to all sorts of problems that arise.

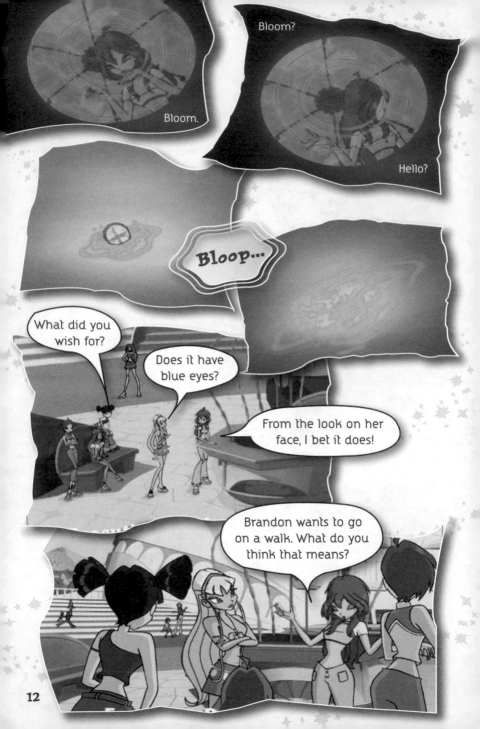

Yo, B! I don't know what going on a walk means on Earth. But in my realm, when your crush asks you out, we usually call it a date!
Well, she can't go. He asked her less than 72 hours in advance.
He's just being spontaneous, Stella.
Actually, I have to agree with Stella. Spontaneity is overrated. Advance planning is a sign of respect.

Well, pretending to have a busy social calendar is a sign of SELF-respect! Besides, what kind of a cheap date is going on a walk? Walking totally limits one's choice of dating footwear!

It doesn't matter. I *want* to hang out with him.

Ooh la-la! It looks like our Bloom is going on a date!

Bloom has a huge crush on Brandon. Personally, I think they make the perfect couple! I just hope she isn't too shy on her date.

They're no fun. But I'm sure you'll do fine.

Fetch!

It's a difficult midterm... Magical Reality.

No way! Did you hear the story about the girl who disappeared in the chamber?

Yeah, I don't think that's true, though.

Tecna says that my performance on this midterm is an accurate prediction of my long-term success at Alfea.

I've seen the kind of power you have. It's awesome. You're totally going to ace your test!

Well, power is only part of it.

I have a feeling you're going to rock!

Oh, I'm going to get so much praise.

Puppy Dog to Stiletto ... the butterfly is flying into the spiderweb. Tomorrow she'll be yours.

Good boy, Riven!

I am sure you've heard quite a bit about this place....

This is it! The Alfea Magical Reality Chamber!

The chamber is the product of the most powerful kind of magic that exists.

Secret ancient spells and potions are combined to create just the right mix of magical energy to produce any kind of virtual situation imaginable!

21

Remember, this chamber creates an entire virtual world. When it's cold, you will really feel cold. And if a rock falls and hits you, believe me, you *will* feel it.

Some like to say the Magical Reality test is what separates the fairies from the pixies!

This is totally you, right?

Yes, it's wonderful!

beep boop
beep beep

Your midterm will be a survival test. The chamber will randomly select a dead planet for you ...

... then it will place you on a virtual version of the planet's surface....

... Here you will have to survive extremely desolate conditions.

23

24

You may bring potion ingredients, but nothing else.

You will have to rely solely on your Winx to survive. As it should be!

25

This is my kind of midterm! All the latest magic and technology Alfea has to offer. I'm sure those witches at Cloud Tower don't have anything as cool as this!

KRAK!

I sent out Knut for the coriandrum sativum...

...he should be back soon.

Then let's warm up. If we do this right, we should be able to astral-project ourselves right into the Magical Reality Chamber!

So we can mess Bloom up without even leaving the dorm!

Let's try it right now!

It's working wickedly well!

Now all we need is the potion and we'll be set to crash Bloom's test. Her power will be ours!

But she has to unleash it so we can capture it. What if she doesn't use the Dragon Fire?

She will, as long as we manage to make her really mad.

If we can't do a simple thing like that, then we don't deserve to be called witches!

Sorry I'm late, traffic was a witch . . .

. . . and I couldn't find any fresh coriandrum sativum. It's out of season.

Wait a minute. Is he talking to those brooms?

Dumb ogre!

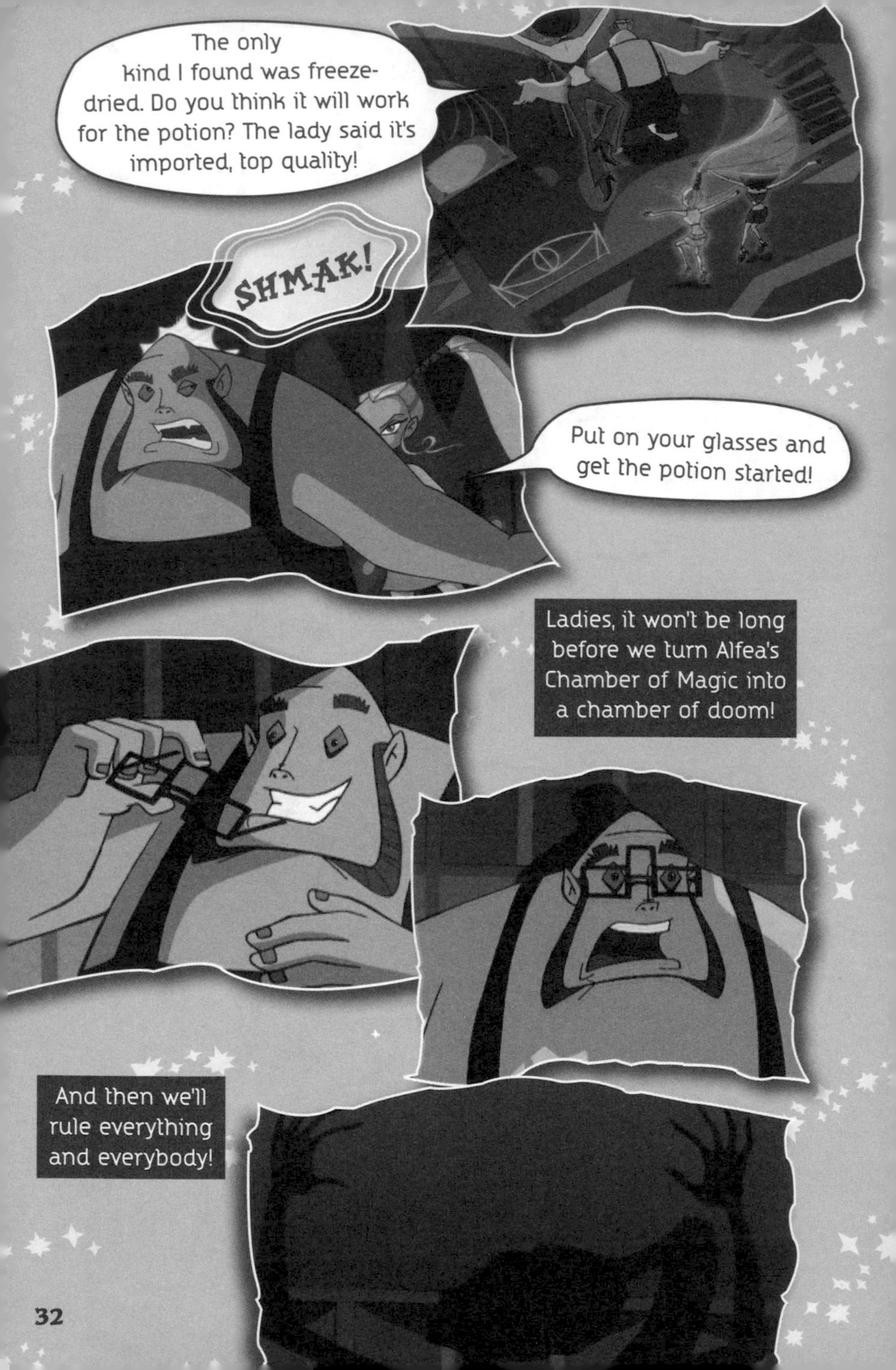
The only kind I found was freeze-dried. Do you think it will work for the potion? The lady said it's imported, top quality!
SHMAK!
Put on your glasses and get the potion started!
Ladies, it won't be long before we turn Alfea's Chamber of Magic into a chamber of doom!
And then we'll rule everything and everybody!

So this is the famous Magical Reality Chamber ... ha!

weeeeaaaaammmmm

Bring to this chamber our witches' magic ... and turn Bloom's midterm into something tragic!

They may be calling this Magical Reality thing a midterm, but for Bloom, tomorrow will be her final exam!

Those witches are always up to something. Why can't they go fly a broomstick or something? They need to leave us fairies alone!

Hmm... I know I saw a protection spell in here somewhere....

...Here it is! *Say this once, say this twice, cast this spell and all will be well.*

Hmm... am I supposed to say the whole thing twice? Or just the second part? Spells are so confusing.

Spells can be confusing. I remember once I tried a shopping spell and nothing went right. Instead of shopping for the perfect purse and shoes, I ended up with clothes that were three months out of style! Can you believe that?

Good morning, class! I trust you are all full of energy and prepared to take your midterm.

I don't feel ready.

I forgot what I studied.

Now remember, this is not make-believe, so be careful. Don't get hurt. Okay?

806512934
268387522
245531689
7

No, I'm ready to go now. I might as well get it over with.
Okay, now remember, you can't leave the chamber until the test is over. But if you are in real trouble, I'll press the emergency button. All set, then?
I guess so. Let me just grab my stuff.
No matter where the chamber sends you, I urge you to trust your instincts.

Okay, Bloom, this will be my last communication with you. Once the environment is set, you'll be on your own.

HUUUMMMMMMM

Huh?

It's really freezing.

43

I guess you can stay.
But right now, I'm going to plant an Eco-totalus tree.
It might not be that tasty but it has all the nutrients we'll need to survive.
And all we have to do is add soil and some Winx, then cast a spell.

Growup acceleratum!

Cool! It's working!

PHOOOOOF!

Look, she's doing *so* well!

Oh, come on! Are you part of the test?

46

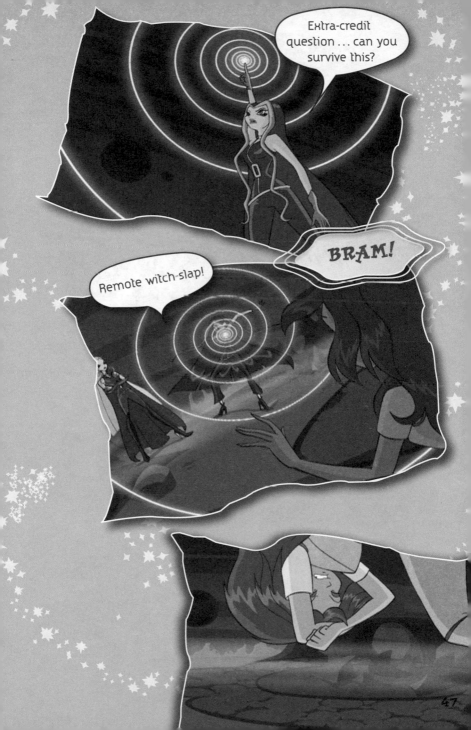

47

I beat you witches in reality, I can beat you here!

You can count on it!

48

49

If I'd known you'd be here, I would have studied my fungus-removal spells!

Get out of my test!

WHOOOOOOF!

Aaaaaaigh!

51

This is so much fun! We should play with dolls more often!
Ready to make her use the Dragon Fire?
The Whisperian Net is set! Let's bait her until she blows her redheaded stack!

And I have the perfect attack to get us rolling....

...Check it out! It affects you both physically and emotionally.

I call it the Cosmic Witch-up!

I think that would go well with some hail and rain!

53

54

FWAAAAP!

You'll end up sorting teeth at the Tooth Fairy warehouse!

SHRRRING!

Ah!

56

57

IIf you don't like the Tooth Fairy warehouse, Cloud Tower could hire you.

You could clean up after the witches!

That is, if you make it out of here in one piece!

58

59

I'd have to rate that a C minus. One more blunder and you'll be failing.

Enough! I've had it with you!

Oh, yeah? You're so weak, you can't even protect your silly little bunny!

Say this once, say this twice, cast this spell and all will be well! Say this once, say this twice, cast this spell and all will be well!

Kiko!

It's a shame. The little bunny was *so* cute.

It's your fault, Bloom. You *did* let it happen.

Bunny-burger, anyone?

HA-HA-HA! HA-HA!

If I were one of those witches, I wouldn't count out Bloom just yet! I'd bet my entire CD collection that she's going to be just fine!

71

A major malfunction, I'm afraid. It's nothing that can't be repaired but I *will* have to postpone the test.

Yay!!!

She aced the test and got it postponed! Give it up for Bloom!

All right, Bloom! Way to go! Woo-hoo! Yes!

Go! Spell it out now! B-L-O-O-M! Wow!

73

Okay, so I aced the test and totally zapped those witches out of there. Not bad for an Earth girl, huh? But I wonder if they really drained my power. Funny . . . I don't feel any different.

75

No one will ever be as powerful as us! We will rule! We will reign! We will run the realm!

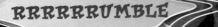

RRRRRRUMBLE

Whisperian Triangle!

NOOOOOOOOO!

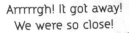

Arrrrrgh! It got away! We were so close!

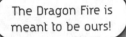

The Dragon Fire is meant to be ours!

And we'll get it, no matter what it takes!

KRA-KOW!

Well, I hope you enjoyed meeting my friends and reliving my adventures. If there's one thing I've learned at Alfea, it's that you never know what's going to happen next. But then again, that's life, isn't it? There's no telling what kind of adventures you may find. And remember, just like me, you never know what kind of power you have inside! Discover your hidden Winx and use it the best way you can!

I'll see you next time. Bye-bye!